PEAK POETRY

A COLLECTION OF PEAK MOMENTS CAPTURED IN POETRY TO COMMEMORATE KIDS AT SCHOOL IN NEPAL'S 20TH ANNIVERSARY

COMPILED & EDITED
BY
KATHRYN BEEVOR

1 3 5 7 9 10 8 6 4 2

First published in 2024 by Kathryn Beevor (Trustee)

Copyright © Kathryn Beevor 2024

All rights reserved. No part of this publication may be reproduced, stored in a retrieval system, or transmitted in any form or by any means, electronic, mechanical, photocopying, recording or otherwise, without prior permission of the copyright holder

This book is dedicated to the memory of May (my beloved grandmother) and Madeline (my kind neighbour, Patrick's mother)

Front Cover illustration by Lucia Sellars
Typeset by RefineCatch Limited, www.refinecatch.com
Printed and bound in Great Britain by Clays Ltd, Elcograf S.p.A

ISBN 978-1-3999-8928-2

Kids at School in Nepal
Registered Charity Number 1111461
www.kasin.org.uk

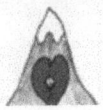

CONTENTS

Sun burns off the mist,
blessing us with heart – warming
heat and love of life
Tony Gould

Introduction	4
PEAK ONE: Nepal	7
PEAK TWO: Rebuilding	15
PEAK THREE: Mountains	23
PEAK FOUR: Nature	34
PEAK FIVE: Peak Moments	43
PEAK SIX: Sport	61
PEAK SEVEN: Diversity	73
Acknowledgements	78
About the Editor	80

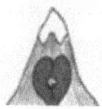

Introduction

Kids at School in Nepal (KASIN) is a wonderful charity which supports the education and wellbeing of young children and secondary students in disadvantaged communities in rural Nepal. It is unusual for a charity as it is run entirely by a small group of volunteers who do not claim any expenses and so all funds raised are given directly to their projects in Nepal.

KASIN has huge support from the Nepali community in the UK. One of their trustees is Prof Padam Simkhada, Associate Dean (International) and Professor of Global Health at Huddersfield University. KASIN also works with Nepali NGO Green Tara Nepal and The Holy Himalaya Trust in Kathmandu.

KASIN was founded by Arthur Benbow who was moved by the poor educational facilities for the children and teachers he encountered in the Kathmandu Valley. In 2003, he returned to England determined to help the loving and kind-spirited Nepalis he had met. KASIN became a registered charity in 2005. Since then, it has helped hundreds of disadvantaged youngsters.

In 2015 a devastating earthquake hit Nepal and the epicentre was not far from Phulkharka where KASIN had been delivering Teacher Training sessions. Almost all the houses and schools were destroyed although mercifully the number of casualties was low as the earthquake happened in the afternoon. KASIN raised funds to rebuild the primary school at Dhandakharka in one of the most marginalised communities and this has inspired the section of the book, Peak Two – Rebuilding.

Since then, KASIN has completed a multitude of other projects: building a hostel for female students to attend a local agricultural college, funding community teachers' salaries, providing teacher training and sponsoring over 80 of the neediest children to attend school in South East Nepal. These children are the first generation from their families to have ever received any formal education.

For the last four years KASIN has been working with Nepali NGO Green Tara Nepal and employing three young Nepali graduates to deliver Teacher Training and Health Education to children in a remote area of Dhading Province. The first phase culminated in opening a Teachers' Resource Centre and providing a dental camp for over 2000 children.

Other projects include running eight after school clubs and these have been shown to be one of the most cost-effective ways of improving education in the poorest communities. For each after school club it costs just £1,500 to provide two teachers, resources and training, six days a week for year. School dropout rates have decreased and exam performance in school dramatically increased. In 2025, the charity proudly celebrates its 20th anniversary and marks the milestone with this book.

More detail about KASIN and the work that it has done can be found at http://kasin.org.uk/

KASIN is always looking for ways to help and hopes you will find the poetry in this book uplifting in the way KASIN seeks to uplift those in need wherever possible.

Kathryn Beevor – Trustee

The proceeds of this book will be donated to KASIN.

PEAK ONE: Nepal

When I wake up – Harihar Timilsina

When the sun sets slowly
The darkness begins to rise
The fireflies come around my home
And shed light on our hearts
When birds return to their nests
Butterflies stop dancing
And flowers, too, cease to sway

The darkness deepens
I can't navigate the way to your heart
I can't discern your face nor see the glow
In your eyes

I feel lonely, tired, and helpless
I try to hear the sound of the silence
I try to feel the resonance of the soul
But I do not succeed in it

I rather hear the sad melancholy of the insects
And the ambiguous howling of wolves
I don't see the mountains, hills, or the rivers
I don't see villages or the fields
I don't see children walking to their schools
Nor the caravans of cattle
However, I see something unusual in my house
There is a fire lit in the hearth,
A tiny star is twinkling in my mind
A few candles are disseminating the rays of faith
And a lamppost is narrating the story of hope

I go to my bed
I close my eyes, postpone my thinking
And start dreaming

I am immersed in a slumber
As if I am dead
I wake up in the dream and feel alive and fresh
I see the light again
I find myself in the middle of the Canola field
Honey bees and birds are dancing

Cattle are grazing
I find a new way of life
When I wake up in the morning
I find a new life every day.

Mother – Kangmang Naresh Rai

Early in the morning swiftly rises
and vanishes the sun in the evening
Over the hill it appears
and down the hill it disappears

Nevertheless, offspring gone away
no return to mother's loving eyes
the way sun light turns up to the courtyard

Stoop body
Craggy countenance
Mother sweeps the main door floor
with the fringe of her patuki
and touches the seeds of seven different crops
on a bamboo winnowing basket

Observing rising sun and setting moon
mother ever keeps waiting
progenies living on foreign land.

Haiku – Tony Gould

(In eastern Nepal)
Round the mountain bend
the road had fallen away
into the abyss

Everest – Justin Coe

Hillary and Norgay's great endeavour
Was to scale the highest heights together
And now their names are known forever
In record books, they've found their place and time
Still many more strive to measure
Their worth against the wildest weather
Everybody has an Everest to climb

Some are born to luck and some to struggle
Some born in riches, some to rubble
Some work hard and some work double
Everybody wants to find their place to shine
Sometimes it takes a lot of trouble
There's years of tears and jeers to juggle
Everybody has an Everest to climb

The road ahead is rising tougher
Sometimes it seems we have to suffer
To reach the peak we must discover
The way to win the battle in our minds
But as storms roar against us rougher
There's strength to find in one another
Everybody has an Everest to climb

We human beings never rest
Always on some epic-quest
To be the quickest or the cleverest
Or simply to survive
Each sunrise sets another test

To beat the blues or be the best
Everybody has
 an Everest
 to climb
And your Everest may be higher still than mine

EVENING – Jane Southward (Trustee)

Golden sun on wooden temple tops
Bells ringing in the gentle breeze
Ornate pagodas rising up from the ground
While we take our ease.
Foreign sounds of Nepalese music
Soothing, relaxing, hypnotic now
Stay this peace, relax in the sun
Watch the day take its final bow
Curtain down as the candles glitter
Incense streams and the pilgrim's chant
Magical, mystical, deeper presence
All is tranquil, it is night

A note from student Ranjita B.K. to KASIN

Respected,

Hello, how are you? I am fine here. I hope you and your family are doing well. I am very happy to write this letter. I want to thank you for helping me in my studies. I have finished my studies. I have finished my pre-school. Now I am ready to join my new school. Thank you for your support and help. Till now take care. Thank you so much. Lots of love to you.

Is this us? – Rfn Laban Pun (1RGR)

I seem to have broken out of my shell,
And I am no longer bounded or lost,
Because I can tell,
By myself, that I have learnt to trust.

I now have no fear to mask
And I know I can fulfil any dream,
Because I have learnt to ask,
Without hesitation, for anything out of my team.

I now am content with just the crust,
And I do not want the full bread,
But everyone getting a piece is a must,
For tomorrow, it's the same needle that we are all going to thread.

I am free from the need to stand out,
And I've found a way to my dream,
Because, now, I have no doubt,
It is being brilliant, just like everybody in my team.

I see the same body and the same face,
And I am trying not to make a fuss,
But I am finding it hard to trace,
For I am questioning, whether or not, we are the same us.

In the words of the poet, he is "remembering the days of my basic infantry training in Catterick (2 years ago). It is about the growth that occurs, in a young Nepalese boy's way of thinking, while learning to be a Gurkha Soldier."

Note: the constant use of the word 'now' is to signify that the thoughts or emotions of trust, bravery, contentment and certainty that exists now, exists because of the unique environment that the training, circle and selection creates.

Oh, For a School – Anon

Amidst the world's vast tapestry unfurled,
Where distant lands with myriad stories whirl,
There lies a realm, the poorest of the poor,
Where children's dreams remain forever obscure.

Oh, muse of mine, inspire my humble pen,
To sing a song for those unseen, unheard by men,
In distant corners of this earthly sphere,
Where education's light struggles to appear.

A land where little feet should freely tread,
Upon the path to knowledge, wisdom's thread,
But poverty's cruel hand does tightly grip,
And dreams of learning for many children slip.

Yet still, hope's beacon burns with steadfast glow,
For knowledge's seeds we desperately sow,
In hearts and minds where dreams begin to stir,
To lift them from the shadows, to freedom's spur.

Each child, a bud that yearns to bloom,
In nature's garden, amid life's gloom,
Their minds, like meadows, vast and green,
Await the rains of learning, pure and keen.

The rivers of knowledge shall gently flow,
Through valleys deep where young minds grow,
From humble huts to lofty peaks they'll climb,
With books as guides, their spirits to prime.

For though they lack the riches that some possess,
Their hunger for learning, none can suppress,
Let's reach across the seas, extend our hand,
And bridge the gap to help them understand.

In unity, we'll write a brighter page,
Empower their minds, unshackle the cage,
So, children in the poorest of terrains,
Shall rise, shall learn, and break their chains.

Oh, let us be like Wordsworth, wise and true,
With verses kindling hearts to what is due,
To educate, to uplift, to light the way,
For every child, regardless where they lay.

Recipe for a festival – Angela Topping

Take some excited people
looking forward
dressed in their best.

Add assorted customs
memories and tales.
Sift carefully.

Include special food
lovingly made
the old-fashioned way.

Prepare to enjoy yourself.

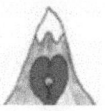

PEAK TWO: Rebuilding

Rebuilding – Oscar Baggett Year 9

In the face of shattered dreams,
We gather strength, or it so seems,
Brick by brick, we start brand new,
Rebuilding what we once knew,

Broken minds and broken hearts,
Rebuilding all the broken parts,
Built with all the broken care,
Trying our best to repair.

Let's embrace the journey ahead,
With it built we will be led,
Rebuilding it piece by piece,
Creating a future of peace.

I Wish – Yuvraj Bhogal Year 8

I am busy
Busy rebuilding my confidence
Confidence which is key
Confidence they don't see
Confidence when I climb a tree
When I swim in the sea
Confidence that I can rebuild.
I wish to be confident
Confident like a Prince
I wish! I wish!

Rebuild – Harrison Andrews Year 7

You can rebuild a home
A place where you live
A place where you feel safe
You rebuild a team

You can rebuild a town or a city
A place with a community
A place with security
You can rebuild a new beginning

You can rebuild a friendship
A friend who helps you on your way
A friend who knows you well
You can rebuild it eventually

You can rebuild love
A friend who you love
A friend who you trust with your life
You can find love again

Rebuilding – Miles Emery Year 8

The night was long
The dark had taken care of light.
It was softly quiet,
Still still, no resolution in sight.

It was cold,
A shoulder unloved the same
Desperately yearning,
For some end of pain.

A drawn-out moment
Where time stood still.
Desperately waiting,
Some end to chill.

Then soon it began,
A single spec at first.
Then brighter quickly,
As the blackness became emersed.

Light shining so vividly,
An opening in space.
Cleasning the dullness,
Some higher divine grace.

Now blazing intently,
The prophecy fulfilled
Whilst time runs in circles
Now a phase to rebuild.

Humanity's Spirit – James Connor Year 7

Admidst the city's symphony
streaks unfold, where the shadows dance,
stories untold.

Beneath lamplights' glow,
a world unknown,
footsteps mark paths,
dreams softly shown,
faces etched with time,
wrinkles define,
in cardboard shelters
dreams align.

In this urban beat,
kindness survives,
humanity's spirit in striving lives,
through trials and feats resilience meets,
a story echoing in these streets.

KASIN – Hugo Watson Year 7

Kind
Amazing
Sweet
Ideal
Nourishing

Rebirth – Thomas Stalder Year 10

Rebuilding, something to embark
When badness leaves everyone in the dark.
From the bottom to the top creates anew,
With kindness and love we push through.

Hour by hour we lay the foundation,
Building God's creation.
Rebuilding the dream that will come true,
Work and more work we will always do.

In each storm that comes upon us
We will find power, working to an end
Hour by hour.

So, we shall collect the pieces one
By one. Rebuilding until we are done.
After it is finished, we shall find our worth,
Rebuilding a new life, a rebirth.

Rebuilding – Leo Jeffery Year 7

In the quiet of the morning
The birds take to the skies,
As the sun rises, a new day is dawning,
A chance to make things right.

If you look up at the night sky,
Amidst the stars shining bright,
You'll see just you and I,
Together, bathed in moonlight.

Rebuilding – Mekhi Burke Year 9

Rebuilding, a journey of strength and grace
A chance to rise to find a new embrace
Through trials faced and battles won
We rebuild like the rising sun.

From shattered dreams we gather the pieces
Building a new hope never ceases
With determination we mend what is broken
Rebuilding our lives words unspoken.

Laying the foundation brick by brick
Forever change the way you fix
Never straying despite the pain
Always staying, more gain.

Just a short time span
Never deviate from the plan
Finish off what you began
Journey continues, promised land …

Rebuilding a journey of strength and grace

The Confidence Bug – Neal Zetter

If you paint it
It will be sunshine yellow
If you drink it
It will feel like fizzy pop
If you meet it
It will keenly shake your hand
If you climb it
You will reach the top

If you eat it
It will taste so sugar sweet
If you hold it
It will give the warmest hug
If you chase it
It will lead you anywhere you want
That's the magic
Of the confidence bug

Rebuilding – Jeevan Mattoo Year 10

We grieve
We build
We restore,
But we do not forget.

All that conflict,
All that torment,
How could we forget?
We have recovered,
Survived,
And moved on.

Will we forget?
I can still feel the pain,
I am still wounded,
My head still aches,
I will never forget.

We grieve,
We rebuild,
We restore,
We reflect.

Being Brilliant – Mark Bird

When someone is good
Just tell them they're good
No woulds. No coulds
No maybe-you-shoulds
No ifs, no buts
No why-didn't-you-puts
No thats, no this
No stars and a wish
No mmms, no sniffs
No much-better-ifs

When someone is good
Just tell them they're good
With whoas, with wows
With show-us-all-hows
With smiles, with cheers
With I love your ideas!

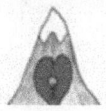

PEAK THREE: Mountains

What Can It Be? – A puzzle poem – Angela Topping

enorMous formations
hOw large they loom
against sUn and sky
blue distaNce
Tall spines
of eArth
ancIent
gigaNtic

theRe for the climbing
And the view from the top
habitats for aNimals
Glimpse from a plane
forever keeping their sEcrets

(Mountain Range)

On Top of the World – Val Harris

Thirteen, barefoot, the day
me and Dad conquered a mountain together,
climbing to the top of Mount Snowdon.

The day I abandoned my blistering shoes,
the day I carried on – onwards and upwards,
barefoot and brave as we climbed higher

through the mist where something heavy
was lifting over the stony ground;
and the less it mattered. The less it hurt.

Me and dad finding new and better footholds.
We sat down to rest where the Llanberis Pass
lay below us. I had never been so high.

I felt like a cloud, resting on the rim of a new
and inspiring view. I wanted to stay forever,
wrapped in the moment – softer, untethered;

my mind seeking better things to say,
my feet and heart singing in the
moment of this deeper harmony.

They cheered us at the top.
Dad took my photo by the peak marker,
barefoot and beaming.

Conquered a mountain,
found a new peak marker for life.

Disabled Steps – Julie Stevens

We can climb mountains
but not like you,
those ropes and harnesses
would weigh us down,
every step for us
takes us higher,
but do you notice?
With burning strength
we set fire to the day,
each flame marks
the lines we cross,
the paths we build
are full of iron,
but do you notice?
These boots don't trek
they pull and heave,
this mind navigates
every single drag,
the summits we find
are near and low,
but do you notice?

Downhill Skier – Thomas Sarahs Year 8

At the top, I felt so happy
I felt so happy, in the sky.
Memories to be made, a good time,
In my adventure, a mountain to climb.

I wait at the top. Breath short
Heart pumping, ready for the launch
I lean forward, defying gravity
And ready

At the hind of the beast
I fleta release,
Then I knew that the mountain,
Was mine.

Skiing- Hudson Baggett Year 6

Swish, swoosh, crunch, crack
It's coming fast down the mountain
Click, clack, it flies by like a cheetah
Hit a bump and lose control
You're covered in snow!
Everyone cheering you on
In the competition.

At the end of the day
Cosy blankets, hot chocolate
To warm you up.

Fresh snow for the next day...

Whimble – Debra Bertulis

Mountains are always there
When you need them
Calling like a ewe to its lamb

Come to me
Let me comfort you
Show you the beauty of this world

It's no coincidence
That when life gives us mountains to climb
We always look for them

And there you sit, still calling
Far away in the distance
Willing us on

Finally, we stumble, breathless
Collapse in a heap at your peak
Gazing out into the wildness

The hardest climb
Rewards with the best view
That can feed a soul for days

Fields, farms, hills one side
Deep rugged valleys to the back of us
Like craters on a lunar landscape

A kestrel soars above
No breeze today
A cloudless expanse all to itself

Today is now a good day
Whatever happens from this moment on
The beauty here says *'it matters not'*

And should you ask me what's on my mind
I'd answer simply *'nothing'*
Nothing at all.

Peak challenge – Sarah Ziman

It's us against the elements
We're ready, standing strong.
We've got our boots, our maps, our packs,
There's nothing can go wrong.

Dad's got the Kendal mint cake
Socks pulled up to the knee,
He's brandishing a walking staff
he's cut from some poor tree.

Mum's bought herself a new cagoule
(Bright yellow, to be seen)
Her pack's got sandwiches and squash,
Her boots are bright and clean.

We're less enthusiastic
(it really looks quite steep)
Still, follow them along a track
more suitable for sheep.

But after only half an hour
my brother's out of puff,
My sister's got a blister
and my legs have had enough.

Dad's tapping at his compass
and says we're heading west,
Mum bribes us with a boiled sweet
and thirty-seconds rest.

It's suddenly got chilly,
The wind begins to blow –
It's like we're halfway up K2
with miles and miles to go.

There's really nothing out here,
Just muddy rock and stones –
Mum's all enthused about the views
(We'd all like working phones.)

But suddenly – more people!
Coming back the other way!
We must be nearly at the top –
Oh, hip-hip-hip hooray!

And all at once we're striding –
It's a race to get there first –
We're grinning and we're winning
and our hearts are fit to burst.

We've reached the pinnacle, the peak –
We did it – well done us!
It's quite amazing up here
(and we hardly made a fuss!)

We add a rock onto the cairn
and gaze out far below,
Mum's right – the view's amazing –
From down there you'd never know.

It's so cool to achieve something
you didn't think you would –
This could be the start of something,
but for now, it just feels good.

Peak – Oscar Wysocki Year 9

On top of the mountain, skies embrace,
Where clouds and dreams can share the same space.
Eagles soar on winds so sleek,
Nature is whispering, no need to speak.
Climbers reach for the summit's peak,
Their hearts are strong, their spirits meek.
Horizons wide, the world seems so small,
From this great height, they can stand so tall.
Each step is a story, bold and unique,
At the peak, where the sky kisses its cheek.

Summit of Life – Henry Busse Year 11

The apogee of life, so sublime.
Perfectly timed melodies synchronize
Joy shines through your face,
A feeling of pure exhilaration.

Mountaintop where efforts climax,
World seems more radiant,
Bathing in the glory of triumph,
Fears and doubts vanish.

Hugging this peak moment
Always close to one's heart,
Savour rare moments with laughter,
Sweetness depends on them.

Cherish these moments as they only happen once,
For in the darkest hour,
There will always be a mountaintop.

Outward bound – Rob Walton

The leaders say we're going
to climb a mountain tomorrow.

I've never climbed a mountain.
I'm scared.

The next day I look
through the curtains
at the dawn.
There's lots of mist
but I can see something
ominous in the distance.

It's big.
Very, very big.

We climb the mountain.
I wonder if they're going
to get us to climb it again tomorrow.

We go to the gift shop.
I buy a key ring and some Kendal Mint Cake.
My friend buys a postcard of the mountain.

The next morning he plays
with the postcard near the window.

I ask him what he's doing.
He says he's taking a peak
through the curtains.

Up and down and up – Rob Walton

I climbed X and saw Y
on the other side of the valley

so I went down the side of the valley
and climbed Y

which is when I saw Z
on the other side of another valley

so I went down the side of one valley
and climbed Z

and then when I looked around
I could see lower peaks

and higher peaks
and even the valley floor

was some sort of a peak
for someone and I thought further

that we all have our peaks
and they're all at different heights

and in different places at different times
and all that really matters

is that we help each other to climb them.

My Two Times at the Peak – Veer Bansal Year 5

When it was winter on the peak,
It was sunny and rainy.
There weren't any people there.
We didn't go up to the statue but I painted some
Chocolate and I liked the Buddha statue.

When it was summer on the peak.
We went on a cable car all the way up.
There were a lot of people there and
We went to a restaurant.
This time we did go up to the Buddha statue.
We went inside the Buddha statue and after that
We had ice cream.

The Peak – Fiona Halliday

The
Peak of
Each mountain
Is hard to reach
Whether in nature
Or our thoughts, deeds or speech
We have times of endeavour
And times when we learn – but we all
Try as we can, until we succeed
Growing together is all that we need!
*(This poem is an etheree, it has a syllable pattern of
1,2,3,4,5,6,7,8,9,10.)*

PEAK FOUR: Nature

Swan's Eggs – Kathryn Beevor (Trustee)

Oval and rare
Stone Age blue
Mother standing
Archaic clusters of
Stash! Yet a promise
One day I will return to
A cygnet bracelet of
Grayscale platinum
But for now, wait
Pubescent you
Each grow
To grace.

The Lake – Chris Morrison BCAo
(Founder of Care Highway International)

A hand is placed on a cool shoulder
somewhere in the middle of a great
storm and suddenly two worlds meet. And
in the distance a train passes by
carrying memories of a lake
somewhere, surrounded by tall grass,
where swans move slowly across the still
silence, and their shadows are
illuminated.
And as the cold light of day arises, he
looks towards the east and the rising
Red Sun.

Haiku – Tony Gould

A noisy skein of
geese flies over my window
in battle order

Stoat on the lawn, its
dance a balletic delight,
pure joie de vivre

Bird – Joshua Seigal

A poem is like a bird.
Words poke their way
through the shell of your brain,
tentatively touching the page

with their baby beak.
You build a nest for them,
feed them worms
so their bones grow strong.

Nursing them diligently,
you protect them from harm.
For a time you mustn't let
anyone approach,

lest their feathers snap
like twigs or their wings
wither and wilt away.
Night, however, turns to day

and with a guarded sigh
you watch your fledgling fly.

Batmagic – Ian Whybrow
(Sunday evening, eight minutes past nine 10th August 2020)

Sewing comes into it,
the suddenly of bats,
the zigzag stagger of their hem stitch
but without the startling warning roar
and drumming on the kitchen table of
my mother's Singer
seventy years ago.

She's here as surely
as the gathering mackerel clouds
on the pink stuff of the sky,
last of the day
between the roof-slope
and the darkening trees
as bats materialise.

No telling where each was
before it is,
the first one simply
      here
and there
      and over there;
a prestidigitation!

Twilight is tacked to night,
myself to boyhood,
in my astonishment
at how some things
were nowhere,
then are wonders
in a moment –
suddenly as bats.

Sky Dance – Linda Middleton

I'm waiting with Grandad…
where the salt sea whispers and softly sighs,
lapping skeletal stilts of the paddling pier.
I'm waiting with Grandad…
where we swallow whole saffron sunset skies
and wonder opens wide our hungry eyes

for the swirling, twirling starling sky dance,
feather-freckling freshly sliced fuzzy peach,
curling, unfurling wide-wandering waves,
spilling and filling the vast ocean stage.
Massing, unfolding, melting and moulding,
rollercoaster dipping, circus flipping,
flying fish leaping, creamy moon sweeping
to catch and snatch the crowd's breath far away.
Teeming, swift streaming, twilight wheeling,
weaving the finest show for work-worn city folk,
swooping low, looping helter-skelter tight
and chattering down for a cosy pier night.

I'm strolling home with Grandad…
old bones, young bones unified, skipping light.
Our minds now colossal kaleidoscopes,
magic shape shifting, starry dream drifting…
anything's possible now…

Author's Note: Starling murmurations are one of nature's most stunning spectacles. These twilight get-togethers between November and March can be seen at various sites in the UK, including Brighton Pier, Sussex.

I want a Hamster – Kavi-Veer Banwait Year 6

I want a hamster
they are cute
they are fluffy
and funny

I want a hamster
They keep you happy
And comfort you

I want a hamster
They sleep
They're energetic
And eat a lot

I want a hamster
They take care of themselves
They burrow
And play a lot

Rainbow Roads – Kayan Patel Year 6

Red: red apples, red books, red hair, red clothes
And red roads.
Orange: orange fruits, orange drinks, orange houses, orange
 pens
And orange roads.
Yellow: yellow rulers, yellow fish, yellow caves, yellow dogs
And yellow roads.
Green: green chairs, green papers, green shoes, green glasses
And green roads.
Blue: blue eyes, blue badges, blue ties, blues ears
And blue roads.

Indigo: indigo shirts, indigo pants, indigo bags, indigo pets
And indigo roads.
Violet: violet hearts, violet mountains, violet sun, violet pencil cases
And violet roads.
Rainbow: rainbow sky, rainbow pool, rainbow shoes, rainbow fields
And rainbow roads.

After Rain, Light – Pie Corbett

The gardens are opals
in a jewellery box.

Cream roses are a pearl rope;
The rose rubies blush.

Flowerbeds are a crush of colour.
A blackbird sings across
the glistening, emerald lawn.
Dawn raindrops are a wedding's promise;
jade leaves hang like ear-rings.
Buttercups are flecks of gold;
lavender, a purple broach;
the morning's glory is sapphire;
fiery topaz sparkles on iris tongues.

The front path glitters,
like a silver chain catching light.
In the distance, the ring road
is a silver bracelet.

The day is a jewel box;
its lid an open invitation.

Where do you come from, Moon? – Carole Bromley
after Charles Causley

Where do you come from, Moon,
to my window tonight?
Will you tell me your darkest secrets?
I might

Do you grow weary, Moon,
do you ever get lonely, like me
and, if so, where do you go?
The sea

What are you made of, Moon,
that you can wax and wane
while I just quietly grow?
We are the same

Do you have friends up there, Moon,
do you talk to the stars?
If you have a favourite, who is it?
Mars

Do you look forward to morning, Moon,
or does it come too soon?
Who are you with your silvery light?
The moon, the moon

Sun Spell – Kathryn Beevor (Trustee)
Sun's response to moon spells

Touchpaper ignites the East,
Criss-cross lines of pink,
Epiphany of first light
Casts a sun spell
Nature's technology.

Moon – white pearl – above
Swaps shifts with the sun
As Sky waters
Into forget-me-not.

Moon's mystique fades
Nightmares of the dark.
Warmth brings early resolutions
Saturating our minds.

At noon's interval, a yellow diamond
Fascinates.
Time for changes
Until arching downwards,
Towards a disappearing act.

Dream dimmed
Lamp lessened
Bonneting the hopes of the day
As the melted gold evaporates.

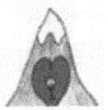

PEAK FIVE: Peak Moments

Classroom Afloat – Kate Williams

I love school most when a lesson comes alive
and the classroom starts to float,
when we're on a magic carpet, sailing away
far and high to... who knows?

I love it so that my skin starts to tingle,
love it from my eyebrows to my toes,
basking in the fizz and the fun and twinkle,
just basking... till the buzzer goes.

Possession – Pie Corbett

Who owns the summer sky?
It is so blue –
surely by now
someone must have laid claim
to such perfection.

Already they've bought up
the earth – whatever next?
Mortgage the wind?
A 'For Sale' notice on the sun?
I gather you can buy a star online;
obsessed by possessions.

Put aside the clutter,
the accumulated years of dust.
There is no need
to own the ivy
that clings to the wall
or the hawk that hangs
above the roadside
like a fluttering cross.

The sun's soft warmth
is there for free –
and the way in which
the snow inscribes the streets.

Even the airplane's
cloudy footprints
enjoy their own beauty.

A Simple Request – Pie Corbett

Not necessarily –
the green-winged orchid
or speckles of winter jasmine
petals in the hedgerow
or the squabble of tawny owls
in Tanner's Wood.

Perhaps –
just a crisp packet's glitter in Farm Lane,
or the snow-crunch of footsteps
or even dust motes
cast adrift in sunlight.

Be curious as a cloud;
those endless shift-shapers.
Notice now, how even the mundane
becomes memorable
when seen afresh.

Why, even a raindrop shines
like a polished tear.

Advantages and Disadvantages – Christine R Milne

There was a big monster from space
who wanted to run in a race.
He was extra strong
and extremely long,
so he came in first and last place.

Camp Life – Mattias Ewing Year 7

You arrive, first day.
Friends? You have none,
But listen carefully to the next word I choose,
As it might just apply to you.
YET,
New people to meet, new friends, new faces!
You end up in new places.
In a forest, woody smell, you are in nature
You might mature,
Awakening in a tent with a yellowish hue,
Surrounded by people, all with you!
After about a week, it all ends,
And you have to say bye to your new friends,
Even if just for a week,
You got a new experience, and hey, that's pretty neat.

Horse Riding – Tom Hipwell Year 9

Horses were scary at first.
They are playful, loving and caring.
Then I felt the power hitting my body.

It's fun to learn about horses.
It's joyful to ride them.
Then I felt the horses gallop as fast as the wind.
When you ride them, you fall in love with them and can't stop loving them.

The Helicopter – Wilfred Shakespeare Year 5

I woke up with a smile on my face
today was the day I could not wait
There was a rumble, a vibration in the air,

the helicopter was coming without a doubt.
Up in the air we went,
all the way to Rottnest.
Below my feet was a bay of diamonds as far as the eye can see.
Every second the island was getting larger and larger,
almost everything we saw was the turquoise sea.
We arrived at the airfield with a bump.
we were here but the ride was over.
Sadly, we had to leave it in the shining sun,
And that was the day I went on a helicopter.

On a boat – Thomas King Year 9

On a boat in Corfu,
Embracing the warm sun,
    As we explore,
The ocean's crystal waters, shades of blue.
A great day of adventure,
Corfu sights to behold,
    This day will never get old.

Dubai Times – Isher Chahal Year 8

The gleaming sun of Dubai
The scorching weather is making me sweat
Fresh crystal, clear seas.
I gazed out of the windows to the breathtaking views
The appetising drinks and scrumptious food.
Dubai really has it all, what does Dubai not have?
Burj Khalifa the world's tallest building
Take a look inside you will be surprised
Dubai smiles to me Dubai
I will visit soon.

I Dazzle like Dawn – Linda Middleton

I dazzle like dawn,
light the way,
soften waves
and brighten the day.
I dissolve shyness,
thaw thick frost,
break the ice
and find the lost.
I curve like a crescent,
shimmer silver stars,
paint blue skies
and fly people far.
I conjure summer,
magic the wag in tails,
comb knots of nerves
and blow breeze for sails.
I float like feathers,
twinkle like tree lights,
splash like an anchor
and bring the twirl of a kite.
I'm canary yellow,
sweet clementine,
the door from the doldrums
and a lifebelt, a lifeline.
I heal heavy hearts
and shine a golden mile.
What am I?
Your sunny smile!

My powers – Rob Walton

At the peak of my powers
I could run a desperately slow mile
in a pair of wellies.

At the peak of my powers
I could watch three shows
on a tablet and two tellies.

At the peak of my powers
I could score a goal
in my own net curtains.

At the peak of my powers
I could say I love you
and know it for certain.

Maybe – Siohban De Mare

Maybe I found you
Maybe you're him
Maybe you're the soul
That my heart can allow in

Maybe you're real
Maybe you're kind
Maybe we can dance
And leave our pasts behind

Maybe you're the sunlight
That I long for, to feel
Maybe your words are genuine
And your beautiful love language is real

Maybe you can feel my heart
Passionate everyday
Maybe you're the smile
That will take all the pain away

Maybe if you are him
You can whisper my name and say
I am that special person
And we can fly away ♥

Our Earth – Fiona Halliday

Spine-tingling moments,
Seeing Earth from space,
Light, atmosphere, Aurora Borealis,
Illumination beyond understanding,
Beauty unrivalled.

Snow-capped mountain peaks,
Breath-catching sights,
Valleys and pastures,
For creatures to graze,
Wonderful abundance.

Awe-inspiring visions,
Water cascading, bubbling, flowing,
Filling rivers, streams and lakes,
Teeming with life, sustaining all,
Our Earth is amazing!

The Reason I Love Raisins – Neal Zetter

What's the reason I love raisins?
Well the reason is they're cool
Like sultanas (not bananas)
Tiny, tasty, squidgy balls

Squashed up tightly in their boxes
Perfect pick from any bunch
Yes I'm really rating raisins
Ripe and ready for my lunch

Raisins, raisins are amazing
Though they're merely shrivelled grapes
Bring the best out of your biscuits
Brilliant if you're baking cakes

I love rapping about raisins
Wrote this rhythmic raisin rhyme
Got a recipe to roast them
With fresh rosemary and thyme

A liaison with a raisin's
Not a thing to ridicule
Because I was raised on raisins
So I reason: RAISINS RULE!

The Magic Box – Aleksander Weir Year 3
After Kit Wright

I will put in the box,

the smell of a winter morning,
an endless bowl of cherries,
my dog surfing on a shark.

I will put in the box,

a knight on the bright moon,
a fairy on a house,
meteors dashing down to Earth.

I will put in the box,

a gloomy night sky,
a star whizzing round Earth,
a giraffe with a pan.

My box is fashioned from,
lava, moon rocks and stars,
with pillows on the lid and chicken beaks in the corners,
its hinges are tiger's teeth.

The Magic Box – Charles Graham Year 3

I will put in the box,

a never-ending slice of pizza,
the smell of bubbly soap,
Santa's amazing magic.

I will put in the box,

a night fury dragon,
a dinosaur's tooth,
a chicken riding a broomstick.

I will put in the box,

my brother's laughter,
my garden in the snow,
a flying hedgehog.

My box is fashioned from,
Lego, diamonds and gold,
With sunshine on the lid and lions at the corners,
its hinges are bones.

The Magic Box – Kareem El – Shirbiny Year 3

I will put in the box,

Cookie's warm kisses,
delicious warm noodles,
endless visits to Legoland.

I will put in the box,

a shark surfing on a tsunami,
a cat riding a broomstick,
Harry Potter's wand.

I will put in the box,

army dogs in suits of strong armour,
a castle with a mysterious dog king,
a scary mouse that breathes fire.

My box is fashioned from,
ice-cream and cookies,
with ice on the lid and fire in the corners,
its hinges are the claws of a cat.

The Magic Box – Oscar Cochrane Year 3

I will put in the box,

Louis' sweet bark,
a flutter of a newly hatched butterfly,
a great white shark.

I will put in the box,

a secret alien,
a roaring monster,
fire from a fierce dragon.

I will put in the box,

an army of marching soldiers,
a castle made for animals,
a strange king on a broomstick.

My box is fashioned from,
fire, water, and ice,
inside there is lots of magic,
but the rest is all dinosaur bones.

The Magic Box – Rayan Shanteer Year 3

I will put in the box,

the sparkle of your eyes on Christmas morning,
a box of never-ending snowballs,
delicious sushi from Japan.

I will put in the box,

the smell of watermelon juice,
fresh summer berries,
a ninja making fluffy pancakes.

I will put in the box,

freshly baked Lego cookies,
a soft cuddle from grandpa,
the first roar from a fierce lion.

My box is fashioned from,
lightening and precious diamonds,
with gold on the lid and reindeer horns in the corners,
its hinges are footballs.

The Magic Box – Angelo Stringfellow Year 3

I will put in the box,

Chinese dragon flames,
a megalodon,
a secret room.

I will put in the box,

juicy, red cherries.
a never-ending slice of pizza,
the smell of cold vanilla ice cream.

I will put in the box,

an army of night dragons,
a baby panda with a pan,
mummy's warm cuddles.

My box is fashioned from,

ice, fire and lightning,
with gold on the lid and steel in the corners,
its hinges are spaghetti hoops.

The Magic Box – Finn Wright Year 3

I will put in the box,

the fur of a snow leopard,
a never-ending box of sushi,
my dog's paw prints.

I will put in the box,

a megalodon surfing on the waves,
the jingle from Santa's sleigh,
a robot flying in the sky.

I will put in the box,

a penguin on a broomstick,
the smell of sweet lavender,
a Legoland hovering in the sky.

My box is fashioned from,
Lego, ice and gold,
with moon rocks on the lid and animals in the corners,
its hinges are dragon's teeth.

The Magic Box – Kabbir Teckchandani Year 3

I will put in the box,

fresh snow on Christmas Day,
a teddy bear's warm cuddle,
aliens from the planet Mars.
I will put in the box,

diamonds from space,
the smell of sweet candy canes,
a puppy's soft fur.

I will put in the box,

the smile from a new born baby,
wizards on a blue lion,
a dinosaur with a bow

My box is fashioned from,

ice, fire and gold,
with clouds on the lid and spies in the corners,
its hinges are the fingernails of pandas.

Year 7 – Luca Ventimiglia-Evans Year 7

I did it, I'm shocked
I finished my first year of High School at the top!
Not top of the class,
Not top in exams,
Not top in sport,
Or any cohort.
But I did my best in everything I could!

I've made new friends,
I've learnt new things,
And I've challenged myself
With everything.

So never say you can't
When you actually can
Be at the top of your own life plan.

Tate Modern – Archer Thomas Year 8

I walk into a building with chequered walls with bricks
The vast lights and expeditions awaited me from a push of
   a lift button
I walked out to see paintings from all colours.
Like a rainbow in the sun of a warm spring day.

I saw and was confused by how the paintings were made
Every single brush was a moment of history from that.
A Person's life is like a bridge to a new world.
Some made me happy, sad, confused but some made me
   laugh.

Sculptures built up from things you would use for daily life
Paper clips, wood, plastic and one was just a pile of sand.
These things had meaning and some had purpose to be in existence.

All these amazing people worked hard on these things.
But it made me think.
We all as humans have the same thing in common.

Art from a significant you.

The Compelling Test – Joshua Horwath Year 8

I was shaking
I was nervous
I was scared
Out of focus
When I looked down
I had a big frown
But my teacher came around
And plopped my paper down
I saw a great big sign
And it looked so divine
It said 96%
Hooray I yelled. I felt as if I'd won the lottery
My friends cheering me
I felt like unstoppable me
A happy ending came eventually

My First Time Playing My Trumpet – Dominic Mallarachi Year 7

My first time playing my trumpet
It was a deafening sound at first
It was enough to make your ears shake.

My second time playing my trumpet
My self-esteem rises when I play the right notes
The triumph of finishing a spectacular piece.

My third time playing my trumpet
The light from my aureate finished instrument
Lures my siblings closer.

My fourth time playing my trumpet
I can smell the grease and effort through the years
Yet my performance still continues.

My Holiday in Italy – Leone Graysmark Year 7

Went to Italy had so much fun
Ate some pizza yum yum yum
Swallowed it whole super tasty
Went into the sea with my broski
Played some footie with a brokie
Beat him well.

What is your peak moment? Share it with a friend and tell them the memories in which you had fun.

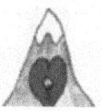

PEAK SIX: Sport

The Baller – Oscar Sandiford Year 9

In the spotlight, the footballer moves with finesse,
Captivating the crowd with skill and precision.
His every step on the field tells a story of dedication and passion,
A tale written in the language of the beautiful game.
With each touch of the ball, he weaves magic,
Creating moments that linger in the hearts of the fans
Long after the final whistle blows.

No way Referee! – Takunda Chademunhu Year 8

No way Referee!
Please don't whine
You'll be just fine
No way Referee

No way Referee
He kicked me in the knee
I am not full with eyes
No way Referee

No way Referee
Maybe you just can see
He clearly hit me
No way Referee

No way Referee
Are you sure it's a foul
Yes of course it is
No way Referee

No way Referee
Well, if I give a foul will you shush?
Yes, we will
No way Referee

No way Referee
'Foul'
C'mon Referee
No way Referee

TIDDLYWINKS – Colin West

If you can't be a world-famous thinker,
You might make a great tiddly-winker.

Peak of Fitness – Sue Hardy-Dawson

Every morning open both eyes
consider the sky (note: always
open curtains before attempting).
While the basin etc. fills, allow time
for aimless drifting, two minutes
for small basin, ten for a whole bath.
Breakfast Recommended: one lightly
toasted sonnet, soft boiled ellipse...
some freshly squeezed ode juice
(note: do not drift during cooking).
Brisk walk lift heart vigorously,
bring: pen, paper, soul, daydreaming
encouraged except if crossing roads
(note: remember to wear suitable clothes)!

Running – Charles Thomas Year 8

I'm summing up my last push
My laces brushing past my foot
Was it worth it?
Am I there yet?

In fields of green, I start to race
Each step I take, a swift embrace.
Through wind and rain, I push ahead,
Running free, no fear or dread.

My heart beats fast, my legs feel light,
As I dash through day and into night.
With every stride, I feel alive,
In this moment, I truly thrive.

The world blurs past, a joyful blur,
As I run and leap, feeling sure.
My worries fade, my spirit soars,
With every run, I find new doors.

Sport – Jake Greasley Year 8

Sport
Sport is entertaining
Everybody likes sport

Sport
It gets your adrenaline going
There are many choices
Cricket with a bat
Rugby with a ball
Football with goals

Sport
You can play all day
You can have fun all day

Sport
Sport is fun

Rugby – James Bannister Year 8

Rugby is about rucking over
Rugby is about tackles
Rugby is about passing
Rugby is about having a good time
Rugby is about working as a team
Rugby is where you have to deem to do well
Rugby is about doing well
Rugby is about doing well as a team

Exercise Bike – Neal Zetter

When building my muscles
And pumping my blood
I never get rained on
Or covered in mud

Exercise bike, exercise bike!
Exercise, exercise, exercise bike!

I'm still where I started
The very same place
Unlikely to win
Any Tour de France race

Exercise bike, exercise bike!
Exercise, exercise, exercise bike!

My two wheels are spinning
As fast as the Flash
But no need to panic
Because I can't crash

Exercise bike, exercise bike!
Exercise, exercise, exercise bike!

There's not any traffic
There aren't any jams
I'm free of all cars
Coaches, buses and trams

Exercise bike, exercise bike!
Exercise, exercise, exercise bike!

Don't want to go swimming
Play football or run
I've found a new way
To keep fit that's more fun

Exercise bike, exercise bike!
Exercise, exercise, exercise bike!

Exercise, exercise
Exercise, exercise
Exercise, exercise...
BIKE!

(PHEW!)

Sport Sport!!! – Elliot Ashley Year 5

Sport! Sport! Goal! Goal!
Into the net it goes.

Sport! Sport! Touchdown!
Now it is one nil.

Sport! Sport! Try.
Now it is on the ground.

Sport! Sport! Wicket.
Now the poles are knocked down.

Sport! Sport! Blow! Blow!
Now the whistle goes.

Swimming Yaseen El-Shirbiny Year 6

One of my favourite sports!
Super, super fun!
Make splashes
Annoy your friends!

I swim like an otter
My sport for so many years!
The crowds cheering me on.

Please, please
Never lose the memories
Please, please pretty please
I won't betray you

Warhammer – Henry Cheetham Year 6

It's plastic
It's got different
Colours it's blue,
Red and others.

It's got a helmet
It's got armour
It's got a chainsaw
And a gun.

It's in a game
It's a character
And it's a
Space Marine.

I would feel sad
It I lose it because
It's one whole part
Of me.

The Game Called Football – Akashdeep Jagdev Year 6

Do you know the game called football?
You see it in the garden, the park and everywhere!
It's black and white
And hexagonal when you strike.
It goes BANG!
If it was not a thing there would be nothing to do
Or watch.
The best moment is when you get it
Straight in the top corner of the goal.

THE ARK OLYMPICS – Clare Bevan

Well, after thirty days afloat,
The animals grew bored –
The Ark just bobbed about all day
While creatures snoozed. And snored.
"We need a little something
To amuse us," someone roared.

But Noah, being clever,
Was ahead of them, and so
He launched the Ark Olympics
With a mighty whistle-blow,
While Mrs. Noah flapped the flag
And shouted: "Off you go!"

The first race was the Marathon
Around and round the deck –
A wrinkled rhino took the lead
Although he looked a wreck,
But then a small giraffe whizzed by
And beat him by a neck.

The next event was 'High Jump'
Which was fun for frogs and fleas
And also bouncy kangaroos
Who won their heat with ease,
While both the desert camels
Grabbed the gold for 'Knobbly Knees.'

'Hide-and-Seek' was battled out
By squirrels, mice and moles,
(Who like to squirm down tunnels
Or to bury stuff in holes.)
The woodlice were delighted
With their prize for 'Forward Rolls.'

The Spiders won the 'Bungee Drop'
With style and speed, of course.
The 'Tail Swishing' medal went
To Dobbin (Noah's horse.)
A MOST annoying parrot won
'Sweet Singing.' What a sauce!

The zebras and the tigers shared
The prize for 'Posh Pyjamas.'
Two snakes inside a basket swiped
'The World's Most Slinky Charmers',
And (yuck!) 'Long-Distance Spitting'
Was a triumph for the llamas.

The elephants, I'm glad to say,
Were best at 'Lifting Weights'.
ALL the monkeys earned gold stars
For 'Juggling With Plates',
An octopus (just visiting)
Won 'Adding Up In Eights.'
By supper time, the animals
Were ready for their beds.
They snuggled in their nests and nooks
And leaky wooden sheds,
As Mr. Noah winked his eye
And: "Well done ME," he said.

Sports That Use Balls – Krish Roda Year 5

You got,
Golf, soccer, football,
Whatever you want to call it,
Baseball, basketball,
Whenever you want to BASH it,
Paddle tennis, tennis, table tennis,
Whenever you want to SMACK it,
Cricket, shot-put,

Whenever you want to BOOM it,
So many sports that use them,
Balls, balls, balls, balls!

Peak Swimming – Sarah Vigne

Determined to swim despite the rain,
I walk in screaming and laughing.

The rain blesses my head,
The waves encourage me.

I take a risk and swim.
I am so free!

Turning over I lie on my back and look at the sky,
I am held by the sea like a baby cradled.
I have given away all my fears.

When Man City Won the Champions League – Jacob Lacey Year 5

The tension
was real. My mum
was on her phone, my
cat was sleeping and my
dad on his laptop. The only people
with their eyes on the tele were me and
my brother eventually I heard the whistle
beep, the game had kicked off, 22 players, 2
bosses and around 8 players on the bench. My mum
tried to catch my attention
but my eyes were
stuck on the
Tele!

First Time – Tobias Reynolds Year 7

Standing on the starting block
My heart was going to drop
Waiting for that starting sound
My heart was ready to pound
If I didn't have this now
How would I be feeling now
In the middle of the race
Everyone quickened their pace
Striving to the end
Driving to the end
Every second not to waste
In this day that I would race.

The Hero – Ethan Carpenter Year 9

In the final of the cup, the tensions were high
With the score at 2 – 1, the game was on the line
But I stepped up to the plate, determined as ever
And vigorously I smashed the ball into the net

The crowd erupted in cheers, my teammates lifted me up
As I sunk to my knees, my heart beat knowing, I had done it
The score was now 3 – 1, the game was won
And I'll never forget this moment

The adrenaline rush, the thrill of the fight
The feeling of victory, bubbling inside me
As in the last few moments my heart thumped against my chest,
I'll carry this moment with me, day and night.

For I am the hero, the one who won the game.

The Race – Attie Lime

The night before
all I could think about was
running.

Not race-running, not
streaming past the lead
to win
by a breath.

Not pounding that track
hard and fast enough
to make me-grooves
in it.

But
away-running
scared-running
I-cannot-do-it
running.

In my sleep
my trainers wore through their soles
my breath was ragged
it rained and it rained and it rained
and still
I ran like I'd trained to run –
I ran and I ran and I ran
and when I woke
I thought

I CAN.

PEAK SEVEN: Diversity

Unique – William Jackson & Leone Graysmark Year 7

The World,
It's not the World without the people,
Differences, distinctions, dissimilarities and more.
They say we are all different after all
Whether you're from Azerbaijan, Japan or Bhutan, Spain
or Bahrain, Indonesia or Tunisia,
El Salvador or Ecuador or even Ukraine.
We are all different, without differences we would not be
unique at all.

The Diversity Stew – Viren Dhaliwal & Leo Jeffery Year 7
After Benjamin Zephaniah

In the simmering pot of diverse beliefs,
Equality stirs gently among differing reliefs,
Buddhism, Islam, Christianity, all in one brew,
Mixing together, no hierarchy in view.

Each ingredient a flavour unique,
In this shared cultural critique.
A stew of unity, where differences collide,
Embracing equality, side by side.

How To Make a Country – Jasroop Ghuman & Arjan Sandhu Year 7

Ingredients:

1 cup of cultures, rich and diverse
2 handfuls of traditions, finely diverse
3 teaspoons of languages, blended with care
4 pinches of customs, unique and rare

Instructions:

1. Begin with cups of culture, varied and bright, mix them gently, ensuring each shines in the light.
2. Add two handfuls of traditions, finely ground, sprinkle them in, let their essence be found.
3. Next, pour in three teaspoons of languages galore, stirring them softly,
4. Lastly, add pinches of customs, distinct and grand, fold them in gently, with a delicate hand.
5. Let the mixture simmer, let flavours unite, in the melting pot of diversity let there be freedom and light
6. Serve with love, understanding, and respect for this recipe, truth we shall collect.

Enjoy the feast of diversity, a recipe ever so fine and kind, where every flavour, every colour, together entwine.

Diversity Matters – Ranvir Gill Year 6

Deposit some Indian women and Chinese men
Into the oven
Heat with a sprinkle of Pakistanis
Then it is spicy.
Mix it up.
Fill with disabilities and put it
In the steaming pot.
Cover the pot with a pinch of skin colour.
Take 50g of equalities, then stir.
Bake it at a warm and cosy temperature for 20 minutes
Eat and enjoy.

Recipe for life – Rhona Stephens

Handfuls of sunshine
A measure of rain
A spoonful of pleasure
A sprinkle of pain

A heart of compassion
A will to forgive
A spirit of kindness
An armful of love

Handle thyme wisely
Be lavish with care
Serve warm with friendship
For best results share

Together – Sebastian Harter Year 7

Although we are so different
Inside we are the same,
Respect traditions and beliefs,
Respect all hopes and dreams.
Let's link together,
And learn from all around,
No need to fight or criticise,
Hand in hand let's harmonise

Year 6 students at Thorpe House School, Gerrards Cross, Bucks, who have supported KASIN through various charity initiatives, May 2024.

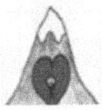

Acknowledgements

There are many people I would like to thank for their support with this book and in no particular order. The comedy performance poet Neal Zetter who sat with me in London to devise a plan in 2023 and who I could always turn to for advice. All the well-known children's poets in the UK and Nepal who have so generously donated unpublished poems so this anthology could be possible. You have now become my friends.

I am truly grateful to the wonderful Gurkhas (serving and veteran) who have shown a keen interest in this book and have provided such insightful words.

I would like to thank Patrick and Liz Wherity who invited me to become a trustee for KASIN in 2023 and gave me the opportunity to compile and edit this book. Thanks also to my fellow trustees, Arthur Benbow, John Peet, Prof Padam Simkhada (also our patron), Jill Deeley, Pamela Ingram, Jane Southward and Mahesh Adhikari. Patrick and Liz have run the charity since 2014 spending many hours on this voluntary work as well as visiting Nepal every year.

Thank you too, to Lucia Sellars who kindly donated her stunning artwork for the front cover which encapsulates the essence of Nepal's beauty and vibrancy.

A huge thanks to my inspirational students at Thorpe House School who have written such heartfelt words of poetry for this anthology – you are incredible and I hope poetry will always be a part of your lives.

Thank you to the production teams at RefineCatch Limited, Bungay, Suffolk and Clays Printers London.

I am indebted to the sponsorship of the charity Care Highway International (Charity No 1119690) towards the cost of the publication of *Peak Poetry*. Thank you for choosing to help our projects in Nepal.

Thank you to my husband Phil, for his patience whilst I have been writing, and who kindly undertook the tireless job of proofreader. Also, my sons Eliot and Calum who have given me the confidence and encouragement to keep going.

Finally, thank you to the amazing children and youngsters in Nepal who make our work so worthwhile.

Kathryn Beevor (Trustee)

About the Editor

Kathryn Beevor is an English teacher, poet, fundraiser and trustee for Kids at School in Nepal. She has raised thousands of pounds for charity – amongst these are NHS charities, Lepra (UK), Teenage Cancer Trust, Heal (Health and Education for All), The Douglas Bader Foundation, Elizabeth's Legacy of Hope, Cancer Research UK, The British Red Cross and Care Highway International. She was a Deputy Head Teacher and has a Licentiate with the Guildhall School of Music & Drama in public speaking.

Kathryn's first poem was published in the book Elizabeth's Poetry of Hope. She writes for children and adults. Many of her poems can be found on the Dirigible Balloon which is a webzine for primary school pupils: dirigibleballoon.org. She is currently working on her own poetry anthology for primary pupils and says many of her ideas are inspired by her students who are also her harshest critics!